MESSER MARCO POLO

Brian Oswald Donn-Byrne
Donn Byrne's life was as paradoxical and romantic as his writing. Although he remained throughout his life a champion of Ireland and its literature, he was in fact an Orangeman, born in Brooklyn in 1889. Their house on Brooklyn Heights, facing New York Harbor, became the focus of the New York branch of the American literary renaissance ("a gang of howling literary brigands" that included Joyce Kilmer and Don Marquis). Almost on publication in 1921, *Messer Marco Polo* brought him considerable fame and fortune. He died in a car crash in 1928, aged 39.

Anthony Lejeune is an award-winning broadcaster, journalist and author. He read Classics at Balliol College, Oxford. He lives in London.

D1009571

Messer Marco Polo

Messer Marco Polo

Donn Byrne

FOREWORD BY ANTHONY LEJEUNE

CAPUCHIN CLASSICS

CAPUCHIN CLASSICS
LONDON

Messer Marco Polo

First published in 1921
This edition published by Capuchin Classics 2008

© Capuchin Classics 2008

Capuchin Classics
128 Kensington Church Street, London W8 4BH
Telephone: +44 (0)20 7221 7166
Fax: +44 (0)20 7792 9288
E-mail: info@capuchin-classics.co.uk
www.capuchin-classics.co.uk

Châtelaine of Capuchin Classics: Emma Howard

ISBN: 978-0-9557312-1-1

FOREWORD

'It's a young man's book,' Donn Byrne's son said to me when I told him that I had loved *Messer Marco Polo* since I first came across it when I was a boy. And he was right. Although ostensibly narrated by a very old Irish storyteller, and despite the fact that its author was himself not particularly young – he was over thirty – when the book was written, it does have a poetic freshness which, like morning dew, is apt to disappear in the heat of life's business.

Byrne's biography can be quickly summarised. He came from a very old Irish family of the traditional wandering fighting kind; two of his ancestors were generals in Spain and in Austria. His father, having an idiosyncratic interest in bridges, had crossed the Atlantic to look at one in the Genesee Valley, so it happened that Brian Oswald Donn-Byrne, as he was christened, was born in America, on November 20 1889. A couple of months later they went back to Ireland, where Brian grew up, mainly in the countryside among people who still spoke the Irish language. At Dublin University he studied Irish literature and Romance languages,

Then he drifted back to America. In New York he made a living, precarious at first but soon quite successful, selling poems and short stories to the magazines.

What he wrote, as the market required, were for the most part war stories and brisk contemporary narratives, while his own inclination tended always to the mistier regions of Celtic romanticism. Among the projects he nursed was the story of Marco Polo, which he had first read in ancient manuscripts at the University. He toyed with the idea of writing it as a poem, then as a play, finally settling on highly coloured prose as the best medium: and at last he found a sympathetic editor, who commissioned it. Putting it into the mouth of an Irish teller of folk-stories allowed him to indulge in historical diversions and anachronisms; for example, he wanted to introduce the poet Li Po, who actually belonged to a different dynasty.

The whole idea does indeed seem very odd – the story of Marco Polo told in an Irish accent! And an accent, simply, is all it is. As his gratified editor observed, not a line of it is written in dialect, and yet such is the artistry of sentence structure, and such a distillation of the spirit of Antrim, that one can hardly read it aloud without attempting the voice of old Malachi.

The whole effect is almost impossible to describe, but the book was immediately recognised by non-realist literary writers, by James Branch Cabell, for example, and later by the Irish politician and diplomat Shane Leslie, as a kind of masterpiece. Brian was now selling everything he wrote, and at very handsome prices: but he and his wife, Dorothea, known as Dolly, whom he had first met at Dublin University and had married in America, lived extravagantly beyond their income. He decided they must go back to Europe. He sold their house in Connecticut for just enough to pay off the creditors, and a magazine editor generously paid him $2,000 in advance. So the family moved across the Atlantic, alternating between England and Ireland, while Brian wrote assiduously and travelled both on the Continent and in the Middle East. Two full-length historical novels resulted – *Brother Saul* about the life of St Paul and *Crusade* about an Irish knight who converts to Islam.

Brian, said one of his friends, 'hated democracy, prohibition, machine civilisation'. He didn't like the modern world nor, though he was certainly an Irish nationalist, did he like what Ireland was becoming. He liked fishing and boxing and horses and gambling, and he rented an old castle beside the sea in County Cork. One night in Cannes he won more than £2,000 at the Casino's high table: he used the money to buy Coolmain Castle outright. As Shane Leslie remarked, many an Irish castle had been lost at the gaming tables but the reverse procedure was unusual.

For the last seven years of his life he was quite well off and enjoyed himself to the full. One night in 1926, just after he bought Coolmain, he went for a drive before dinner. Dolly said she was too tired to go with him. He never returned. His car, which proved to have defective steering, pitched off the road into the wild waters of Courtmacsherry Bay at high tide.

Of the considerable body of work which Donn Byrne produced in a relatively short life the Irish stories keep their particular admirers and *Brother Saul* is a fine book, but there can be no doubt that *Messer Marco Polo* will always be his best remembered, his unique, achievement. The historically curious may ask: how much does it resemble the true story of Marco Polo? And the perhaps surprising answer is – quite closely.

That Marco Polo did what he said he did and in general saw what he said he saw has never been very seriously questioned. The claim, in the prologue to his own book, that its author had travelled more widely than any other man since the Creation, was, as far as written records are concerned, plain fact. In the year 1271, aged seventeen, he set out with his father and uncle for China, served Kubla Khan in various roles, travelled widely in Central Asia, visited India and Burma, and after twenty years returned, almost unrecognisable but laden with jewels, to Venice. When subsequently he was made a prisoner-of-war in Genoa he met a romance writer named Rustichello. They sent for Marco's notes and, between them, compiled the narrative of his travels. No copy of the original text, which was probably in French, survives, but several almost contemporary copies, in various languages (including, as it happens, Irish) do. The love story in *Messer Marco Polo* is Donn Byrne's invention, but much else – the visit to the Pope, for example, and the tale of the Old Man of the Mountain and his assassins – come straight out of the Polo-Rustichello book.

A good deal has quite recently been confirmed from Chinese sources, Did Marco and Rustichello, and in due course Donn

Byrne, exaggerate from time to time, did they embellish their anecdotes a little here and there? Of course they did. What far-traveller from Herodotus onwards has ever failed to do so? Does it matter? Not a scrap. The important thing is that Marco Polo's great book has here inspired a wonderful small book. 'Young men see visions and old men dream dreams.' These are what matter, not the prosaic accidents of historic truth.

Anthony Lejeune
London, May 2008

MESSER MARCO POLO

The message came to me, at the second check of the hunt, that a countryman and a clansman needed me. The ground was heavy, the day raw, and it was a drag, too fast for fun and too tame for sport. So I blessed the countryman and the clansman, and turned my back on the field.

But when they told me his name, I all but fell from the saddle. "But that man's dead!"

But he wasn't dead. He was in New York. He was travelling from the craigs of Ulster to his grandson, who had an orange-grove on the Indian River, in Florida. He wasn't dead. And I said to myself with impatience, "Must every man born ninety years ago be dead?"

"But this is a damned thing," I thought, "to be saddled with a man over ninety years old. To have to act as *garde-malade* at my age! Why couldn't he have stayed and died at home? Sure, one of these days he will die, as we all die, and the ghost of him will never be content on the sluggish river, by the mossy trees, where the blue herons and the white cranes and the great gray pelicans fly. It will be going back, I know, to the booming surf and the red-berried rowan-trees and the barking eagles of Antrim. To die out of Ulster, when one can die in Ulster, there is a grey foolish thing . . ."

But the harsh logic of Ulster left me, and the soft mood of Ulster came on me, as I remembered him, and I going into the town on the train. And the late winter grass of Westchester, spare, scrofulous; the jerry-built bungalows; the lines of uncomely linen; the blatant advertising boards—all the unbeauty of it passed away, and I was again in the Antrim glens. There was the soft purple of the Irish Channel, and there the soft, dim outline of Scotland. There was the herring school silver in the sun, and I could see it from the crags where the surf boomed like a drum. And underfoot was the heather, the springy heather, the belled and purple heather . . .

And there came to me again the vision of the old man's thatched farmhouse when the moon was up and the bats were out, and the winds of the County Antrim came bellying down the glens . . . The turf fire burned on the hearth, now red, now yellow, and there was the golden light of lamps, and Malachi of the Long Glen was reciting some poem of Blind Raftery's, or the lament of Pierre Ronsard for Mary, Queen of Scots:

Ta ribin o mo cheadshearc ann mo phoca sios.
Agas mna Eirip ni leigheasfadaois mo bhron, faraor!
Ta me reidh leaf go ndeantar damh comhra caol!
Agas gobhfasfaidh an fear no dhiaidh sin thrid mo lar anios!

There is a ribbon from my only love in my pocket deep,
And the women of Europe they could not cure my grief, alas!
I am done with you until a narrow coffin be made for me.
And until the grass shall grow after that up through my heart!

And I suddenly discovered on the rumbling train that apart from the hurling and the football and the jumping of horses, what life I remembered of Ulster was bound up in Malachi Campbell of the Long Glen . . .

A very strange old man, hardy as a blackthorn, immense, bowed shoulders, the face of some old hawk of the mountains, hair white and plentiful as some old cardinal's. All his kinsfolk were dead except for one granddaughter . . . And he had become a tradition in the glens . . . It was said he had been an ecclesiastical student abroad, in Valladolid, . . and that he had forsaken that life. And in France he had been a tutor in the family of

MacMahon, *roi d' Irlande*, . . and somewhere he had married, and his wife had died and left him money. . . and he had come back to Antrim . . . He had been in the Papal Zouaves, and fought also in the American Civil War . . . A strange old figure who knew Greek and Latin as well as most professors, and who had never forgotten his Gaelic . . .

Antrim will ever colour my own writing. My Fifth Avenue will have something in it of the heather glen. My people will have always a phrase, a thought, a flash of Scots-Irish mysticism, and for that I must either thank or blame Malachi Campbell of the Long Glen. The stories I heard, and I young, were not of Little Rollo and Sir Walter Scott's, but the horrible tale of the Naked Hangman, who goes through the Valleys on Midsummer's Eve; of Dermot, and Granye of the Bright Breasts; of the Cattle Raid of Maeve, Queen of Connacht; of the old age of Cuchulain in the Island of Skye; grisly, homely stories, such as yon of the ghostly footballers of Cushendun, whose ball is a skull, and whose goal is the portals of a ruined graveyard; strange religious poems, like the Dialogue of Death and the Sinner:

Do thugainn loistin do gach deoraidh treith-lag—
I used to give lodging to every poor wanderer;
Food and drink to him I would see in want,
His proper payment to the man requesting reckoning,
Och! Is not Jesus hard if he condemns me!

All these stories, of all these people he told, had the unreal, shimmering quality of that mirage that is seen from Portrush cliffs, a glittering city in a golden desert, surrounded by a strange sea mist. All these songs, all these words he spoke, were native, had the same tang as the turf smoke, the Gaelic quality that is in dark lakes on mountains summits, in plovers nests amid the heather . . . And to remember them now in New York, to see him . . .

Fifteen years had changed him but little: a little more tremor and slowness in the walk, a bow to the great shoulders, an eye that flashed like a knife.

"And what do you think of New York, Malachi?"

"I was here before, your honour will remember. I fought at the Wilderness."

I forbore asking him what change he had found. I saw his quivering nostrils.

In a few days he would proceed south, when he had orientated himself after the days of shipboard.

That night it seemed everyone chose to come in and cluster around the fire. Randall, the poet; and the two blonde Danish girls, with their hair like flax; Fraser, the golfer, just over from Prestwick; and a young writer, with his spurs yet to win; and this one . . . and that one.

They all kept silence as old Malachi spoke, sportsmen, artists, men and women of the world; a hush came on them, and their eyes showed they were not before the crackling fire in the long room, but amazed in the Antrim glens.

Yes, old Malachi said, things were changed over there, and a greater change was liable . . . People whispered that in the Valley of the Black Pig the Boar without Bristles had been seen at the close of the day, and in Templemore there was a bleeding image, and these were ominous portents . . . Some folks believed and some didn't . . . And the great Irish hunter that had won the Grand National, the greatest horse in the world . . . But our Man of War, Malachi? . . Oh, sure, all he could do was run, and a hare or a greyhound could beat him at that; but Shawn Spadah, a great jumper him, as well as a runner; in fine, a horse. . . And did I know that Red Simon McEwer of Cushundall had gone around Portrush in eighteen consecutive fours?. . A Rathlin Islander had tried the swim across to Scotland, but didn't make it, and there was great arguing as to whether it was because of the currents or of lack of strength. . . There were rumblings in the

Giants' Causeway . . . very strange . . . A woman in Oran had the second sight, the most powerful gift of second sight in generations . . . There was a new piper in Islay, and it was said he was a second McCrimmon . . . And a new poet had arisen in Uist, and all over the Highlands they were reciting his songs and his "Lament for the Bruce". . . Was I still as keen for, did I still remember the poems, and the great stories? . .

" 'Behold, the night is of great length,' " I quoted, " 'Unbearable. Tell us, therefore, of those wondrous deeds.' "

"If you've remembered your Gaidhlig as you've remembered your Greek!"

"It's a long time since you've had a story of me, twelve long years, and it's a long time before you'll have another, and I going away tomorrow. Old Sergeant Death has his warrant out for me this many a day, and it's only the wisdom of an old dog fox that eludes him; but he'll lay me by the heels one of these days, . . then there'll be an end to the grand stories . . . So after this, if you're wanting a story, you must be writing it yourself . . .

"But before I die, I'll leave you the story of Marco Polo. There's been a power of books written about Marco Polo. The scholars have pushed up their spectacles and brushed the cobwebs from their ears, and they've said, 'There's all there is about Marco Polo.'

"But the scholars are a queer and blind people, Brian Oge. I've heard tell there's a doctor in Spain can weigh the earth. But he can't plow a furrow that is needful for planting corn. The scholars can tell how many are the feathers in a bird's wing, but it takes me to inform the doctors why the call comes to them, and they fly over oceans without compass or sextant or sight of land.

"Did you ever see a scholar standing in front of a slip of a girl? In all his learning he can find nothing to say to her. And every penny poet in the country knows.

"Let you be listening now, Brian Oge, and let also the scholars be listening. But whether the scholars do or not, I 'm not caring.

A pope once listened to me with great respect, and a marshall of France and poets without number. But the scholars do be turning up their noses. And, mind you, I've got as much scholarship as the next man, as you'll see from my story.

"Barring myself, is there noone in this house that takes snuff? No! Ah, well, times do be changing."

I

Now it's nearing night on the first day of spring, and you could see how loath day was to be going for even the short time until the rising of the sun again. And though there was a chill on the canals, yet there was great colour to the sunset, the red of it on the water ebbing into orange, and then to purple, and losing itself in the olive pools near the mooring-ties. And a little wind came up from the Greek islands, and now surged and fluttered, the way you'd think a harper might be playing. You'd hear no sound, but the melody was there. It was the rhythm of spring, that the old people recognise.

But the young people would know it was spring, too, by token of the gaiety that was in the air. For nothing brings joy to the heart like the coming of spring. The folk who do be blind all the rest of the year, their eyes do open then, and a sunset takes them, and the wee virgin flowers coming up between the stones, or the twitter of a bird upon the bough . . . And young women do be preening themselves, and young men do be singing, even they that have the voices of rooks. There is something stirring in them that is stirring in the ground, with the bursting of the seeds . . .

And young Marco Polo threw down the quill in the counting house where he was learning his trade. The night was coming on. He was only a strip of a lad, and to lads the night is not rest from work, and the quietness of sleeping, but gaming and drinking, and courting young women. Now, there were two women he might have gone to, and one was a great Venetian lady, with hair the red of a queen's cloak, and a great noble shape to her and great dignity. But with her he would only be reciting verses or making grand, stilted compliments, the like of those you would hear in a play. And while that seemed to fit in with winter and candlelight, it was poor sport for spring. The other one was a black, plump little gown-maker, a pleasant, singing little woman, very affectionate, and very proud to have one of the great Polos loving her. She was eager for kissing, and always asking the lad to be careful of himself, to be putting his cloak on, or to be sure and drink something warm when he got home that night, for the air from the canals was chill. The great lady was too much of the mind, and the little gownmaker was too much of the body, either of them, to be pleasing young Marco on the first night of spring.

Now, it is a queer thing will be pleasing a young man on the first night of spring. The wandering foot itches, and the mind and body are keen to follow. There is that inside a young man that makes the hunting dog rise from the hearth on a moonlight night: "Begor! it's myself'll take a turn through the fields on the chance of a bit of coursing. A weasel, maybe, or an otter, would be out the night. Or a hare itself. Ay, there would be sport for you! The hare running hell-for-leather, and me after him over brake and dell. Ay! Ay! Ay! a good hunt's a jewel! I'll take a stretch along the road."

Or there is in him what does be troubling the birds, and they on tropic islands. "Tweet-tweet," they grumble. "A grand place this surely, and very comfortable for the winter. The palm trees are green, but I'd rather have the green of young grass. And the sea, you ken, it becomes monotonous. Do you remember the peaches of Champagne, wife, and the cherry trees of Antrim? Do you remember the farmer who was such a bad shot, and his wife with the red petticoat? I'm feeling fine and strong in the wings, *avourneen*. What do you say? Let's bundle and go!"

He wandered out with the discontent of the season on him. The sun had dropped at last, and everywhere you'd see torches, and the image of torches in the water. On the canals of the town great barges moved. Everywhere were fine, noble shadows and the splashing of oars. There was a great admiral's galley, ready to put to sea against Genoa. There a big merchantman back from Africa. And along the canals went all the people in the world, you'd think. Now it was a Frenchman, all silks and satins and *"la-di-da, monsieur!"* Or a Spaniard with a pointed beard and long, lean legs and a long, lean sword. And now it was a Greek courtesan, white as milk, sitting in her gondola as on a throne. Here was a Muscovite, hairy, dirty, with fine fur and fine jewels and teeth sharp as a dog's. And now an effeminate Greek nobleman, languid as a bride. And here were Moorish captains, *Othello's* men, great giants of black marble; and swarthy, hook-nosed merchants of Palestine; and the squires of Crusaders—pretty, ringleted boys, swearing like demons. And here and there were Scots and Irish mercenaries, kilted, sensitive folk, one moment smiling at you and the next a knife in your gizzard.

And as he went through the courts there were whispers and laughter, and occasionally a soft voice invited him to enter; but he smiled and shook his head.

Near the Canal de Mestre, which is close by the Ghetto, he stopped by the wine shop called The Prince of Bulgaria, and he could hear great disputation. And some were speaking of Baldwin II, and how he had no guts to have let Palæologus take Constantinople from him. And others were murmuring about Genoa. "Mark us, they mean trouble, those dogs. Better wipe them off the face of the earth now." And a group were discussing the chances of raiding the Jewish Kingdom of the Yemen. "They've got temples there roofed with gold". . . And an Irish piper was playing on a little silver set of pipes, and an Indian magician was doing great sleight of hand . . .

"I'll go in and talk to the strange foreign people," said Marco Polo.

II

Now, you might be thinking that the picture I'm drawing is out of my own head. Let you not be thinking of it as it is now, a city of shadows and ghosts, with a few scant visitors mooning in the canals. The Pride of the West she was, the Jewel of the East. Constantinople was her courtyard. Greece, Egypt, Abyssinia, Bulgaria, and Muscovy, her ten acre fields. The Crusaders on their way to fight the Saracen stopped to plead for her help and generosity. There were no soldiers more chivalrous, not even the French. There were no better fighters, not even the Highland clans. Sailors? You'd think those fellows had invented the sea. And as for riches and treasures, oh! the wonder of the world she was. Tribute she had from everywhere; the four great horses of Saint Mark they came from Constantinople. The two great marble columns facing the Piazetta, sure, they came from Acre. When foreign powers wanted the loan of money, it was to Venice they came. Consider the probity of Venetian men. They once held as pledge the Crown of Thorns itself. King Louis IX of France redeemed it.

The processions of the tradespeople were like a king's retinue, and they marching in state on the election of a doge. Each in their separate order they'd come, the master smiths first, as is right, every one garlanded like a conqueror, with their banner and their buglers. The furriers next in ermine and taffeta; the tanners, with silver cups filled with wine; the tailors in white, with vermilion stars; the wool-workers, with olive branches; the quiltmakers in cloaks trimmed with fleur-de-lys ; the cloth-of-gold weavers, with golden crowns set with pearls; the shoemakers in fine silk, while the silk-workers were in fustian; the cheese-dealers and pork-butchers in scarlet and purple; thefish-mongers and poulterers, armed like men-of-war; the glass-makers, with elegant specimens of their art; the comb-makers, with little birds in cages; the barber-surgeons on horseback, very dignified, very learned, and with that you'd think there'd be an end to them, but cast your eye back on that procession and you'd find guilds as far as your sight would reach ...

Let you be going down the markets, and what would you see for sale? Boots, clothes, bread? No, they were out of sight; but scattered on the booths, the like of farls of bread on a fair-day, you'd find cloves and nutmegs, mace and ebony from Moluccas, that had come by way of Alexandria and the Syrian ports; sandalwood from Timor, in Asia; camphor from Borneo. Sumatra and Java sent benzoin to her markets. Cochin China sent bitter aloes-wood. From China and Japan and from Siam came gum, spices, silks, chessmen, and curiosities for the parlour. Rubies from Peru, fine cloths from Coromandel, and finer still from Bengal. They got spikenard from Nepal and Bhutan. Their diamonds were from Golconda. From Nirmul they purchased Damascus steel for their swords. Nor is that all you'd see, and you'd be going down by the markets on a sunny morning, and a fine-thinking, low-voiced woman on your arm. You'd see pearls and sapphires, topaz and cinnamon from Ceylon; lac and agates, brocades and coral from Cambay; hammered vessels and inlaid weapons and embroidered shawls from Cashmere. As for spices, never would your nostrils meet such an odor: bdellium from Scinde, musk from Tibet, galbanum from Khorasan; from Afghanistan, asafetida; from Persia, sagapenum; ambergris and civet from Zanzibar, and from Zanzibar came ivory, too. And from Zeila, Berbera, and Shehri came balsam and frankincense ...

And that was Venice, and Marco Polo a young man. And now it's only a town like any other town but for its churches and canals. There's many a town has ghosts, but none the ghosts that Venice has; not Rome itself, or Tara of the kings.

"Once did she hold," Randall quoted, "the gorgeous East in fee;
And was the safeguard of the West; the worth
Of Venice did not fall below her birth,
Venice, the eldest Child of Liberty.
She was a maiden city, bright and free;
No guile seduced, no force could violate;
And, when she took unto herself a mate,
She must espouse the everlasting Sea!"

Time is the greatest rogue of all. Not all the arrows of Attila can do the damage of a trickle of sand in an hour-glass in Tyre and Sidon, Carthage, ancient Babylon, and Venice, queen of them all.

I am describing Venice to you for this reason. You might now stand where Troy's walls once were and say to yourself: "Was this where Helen walked with her little son? Was this where the loveliest face of ages wept?" And a chill of doubt would come on you, and you would think, "I've been wasting my sorrow and wasting my love, for it was all nothing but an old tale made up in a minstrel's head."

And sometime in Venice, after your dinner in a hotel, you'd go out for a while in a *barca*, that would have no more romance to it nor the bark a gillie would row, and you salmon-fishing on a cold, blustery day, and you would feel disappointed, you having come so far, and you'd say: "It was a grand story surely, and bravely did it pass the winter evening; but wasn't old Malachi of the Long Glen the liar of the world!"

I wouldn't have you saying that, and I dead. In all I'm telling you, I'd have you to know there's not a ha'pen'orth of lie.

III

And so Marco Polo went into the wine shop to see and hear the strange foreign people.

It was a dark, long room, very high, full of shadows between the flaming torches on the wall. At one side of it was a great fire burning, for all it was the first night of spring. At one end of it were the great barrels of liquor for the thirsty customers; black beer for the English and the Irish, grand, hairy stuff with great foam to it, and brown beer for the Germans; and there was white wine there for the French people, and red wine for the Italians, asquebaugh for the Scots, and rum from the sugar cane for such as had cold in their bones. There was all kind of drink there in the brass-bound barrels—drink would make you mad and drink would make you merry, drink would put heart in a timid man and drink would make fighting men peaceful as pigeons; and drink that would make you forget trouble—all in the brass-bound barrels at the end of the room. And pleasant, fat little men were roaming around serving the varied liquor in little silver cups, and fine Venetian glasses for the wine, and in broad-bellied drinking-pots that would hold more than a quart.

And there was such a babel of language as was never heard but in one place before.

Some of the drinkers were dicing and shouting as they won, and grumbling and cursing when they lost. And some were singing. And some were dancing to the Irish pipes. And there was a knot around the Indian conjurer.

But there was one man by himself at a table. And him being so silent, you'd think he was shouting for attention. He was so restful against the great commotion, you'd know he was a great man. You might turn your back on him, and you'd know he was there, though he never even whispered nor put out a finger. A fat, pleasant, close-coupled man he was, in loose, green clothes, with gold brocade on them. And there were two big gold earrings in his lobes. He smoked a wee pipe with the bowl half-ways up it. The pipe was silver and all stem, and the bowl no bigger than a ten-cent piece. His shoulders were very powerful, so you'd know he was a man you should be polite to, and out of that chest of his a great shout could come. He might have been a working man, only, when he fingered his pipe, you'd see his hands were as well kept as a lord's lady's, fine as silk and polished to a degree. And you'd think maybe a pleasant poet, which is a scarce thing, until you looked at the brown face of him and big gold earrings. And then you'd know what he was: he was a great sea-captain.

But where did he come from? You might know from the high cheek bones and the eyes that were on a slant, as it were, that it was an Eastern man was in it. It might be Java and it might be Borneo, or it might be the strange country of Japan.

And there were a couple of strange occurrences in the wine shop. The Indian juggler was being baited by the fighting men, as people will be after poking coarse fun at a foreigner. The slim Hindu fellow wasn't taking it at all well. He was looking with eyes like gimlets at a big bullock of a soldier that was leading the tormenters.

"Show me something would surprise me," he was ordering. "Be damned to this old woman's entertainment!" says he. "As a magician," says he, "you're the worst I ever saw. If you're a magician," says he, "I'm a rabbit."

And there was a roar at that, because he was known to be a very brave man.

"Show me a magic trick," says he.

Says the Hindu:

"Maybe you'd wish you hadn't seen it."

"Be damned to that!" says the big fellow.

"Look at this man well," the Hindu told the room. "Look at him well." He throws a handful of powder in the fire and chants in his foreign language. A cloud of white smoke arises from the fire. He makes a pass before it, and, lo and behold ye! it's a screen against the wall. And there's a great commotion of shadows on the screen, and suddenly you see what it's all about. It's a platform, and a man kneeling, with his head on the block. You don't see who it is, but you get chilled. And suddenly there's a headsman in a red cloak and a red mask, and the ax swings and falls. The head pops off, and the body falls limp. And the head rolls down the platform and stops, and you see it's the head of the fellow who wanted to see something, and it's in the grisly grin of death . . .

"There's your latter end for you," says the conjurer. "You wanted to see something. I hope you're content."

The big fellow turns white, gulps, gives a bellow, and makes a rush; but the conjurer isn't there, nor his screen nor anything.

Everybody in the room was white and shaken—all but the sea-captain. He just tamps his pipe as if nothing had happened, and smokes on. He doesn't even take a drink from his glass.

And a little while later an Irish chieftain walks in. He's poor and ragged and very thin. You might know he'd been fighting the heathen for the Holy Sepulchre, and so entitled to respect, no matter what his condition. And behind him are five clansmen as ragged as he. But a big German trooper rolls up.

"And what are you?" says the big, burly fellow.

"A gentleman, I hope," says the ragged chief.

" 'Tis yourself that says it," laughs the German trooper. The chieftain snicks the knife from his armpit, and sticks him in the jugular as neat as be damned.

"You'd might take that out, Kevin Beg"—the Irish chief points to the killed man—"and throw it in the canal. Somebody might stumble over it and bark their shins."

Now this, as you can conceive, roused a powerful commotion in the room. They were all on their feet, captains and mariners and men-at-arms, cheering or grumbling, and arguing the rights and wrongs of the matter. All but the sea-captain, who saw it all, and he ever blinked an eyelid, never even missed a draw of the pipe.

And then Marco Polo knew him to be a Chinaman, because, as all the world knows, Chinamen are never surprised at anything.

IV

So Marco Polo goes over and salutes him politely. "I wonder if you mind my sitting down by you for a while," he says. "I perceive you're from China."

The sea-captain waves him politely to his place.

"I'm from China." He smiles. "You guessed right."

"Is it long since you've been in China?"

"Well, that depends upon what you call long," says the captain. "If you mean time," it's one thing. If you mean voyage, it's another. For you've got to take into account," says he, "adverse winds, roundabout turns to avoid currents, possible delays to have the ship scraped free from the parasite life that does be attaching itself to the strakes, time spent in barter and trade. Other matters, too; the attacks of pirates; cross-grained princes who don't want you to be leaving their ports with a good cargo in your hold; sickness; loss of sails and masts; repairs to the ship. It wasn't a short journey and it wasn't a long one."

"It will be a long ways to China, I'm thinking."

"I can tell you how long it is from China to here, and you can reverse that, and you will get a fair idea of how long it is from here to China. I left Zeitoon with a cargo of porcelain for Japan, and traded it for gold-dust, and from Japan I went to Chamba to lay in a store of chessmen and pen-cases. And from Chamba I sailed to Java, which is the greatest island in the world. Java is fifteen hundred miles from Chamba, south and southeast, and it took me four months sailing, but a sea-captain cannot pass Java by, for it is the chief place for black pepper, nutmegs, spikenard, galingale, cubebs, cloves, and all the spices that grow.

"And I stopped at various small islands from there, until I came to Basma, which is the island of the unicorns. And there we trade in pygmies, which ignorant people think are human folk. They are just a wee monkey, with all the hair plucked out except the hair of the beard. There is great money in them.

"I stopped at Sumatra for coconuts and toddy, and just for water at Dragoian. Dragoian is not a good city. It is filled with sorcerers who have tattooed faces. At Lambri I put in for the sago you buy from the hairy men with tails.

"Son, never stop at the isle of Andaman. The men there have faces like dogs. They are a cruel generation, and eat every one they can catch. I could tell you a story, but I would not spoil this fine spring night. Go rather to the island of Ceylon, and see the King's Ruby, which is the greatest jewel in the world. I stopped there and at Coromandel for the pearls the divers go down in the sea for, and there are no clothes on that island, so that every one goes naked as a fish. And there is the shrine of Saint Thomas. I was there.

"Gujarat, Tana, I stopped there. The Male and Female Islands I put into for ambergris. Svestra, which is full of magicians—I was there, too. Madagascar and Zanzibar, where they live on camel flesh, I was there. And from Zanzibar I came north to Abyssinia, because I had to get an ostrich there for the King of Siam. And there was a letter and a parcel for the Sultan of Egypt. So I went to Cairo. I had a month on my hands, so I thought I'd run over and see Venice, because it's a hobby of mine, you might say, to see the world.

"Now let me reckon. Four and three makes seven, and four more are eleven, and six are seventeen, and let us say nine with that, and you have twenty-six. And the month I'm forgetting on the rocks of Aden is twenty-seven, and a week here and a week there for bad winds and such like. It would be safe to put that at three months. So it's two years and a half since I left China."

"You never," says young Marco, "met anybody in China by the name of Polo?"

"Poh-lo? Poh-lo? China's a bigger place nor you would imagine, laddie. There's half a hundred million people there."

"These were foreigners," Marco explained, "traders. They were at the court of the great Khan."

"Polo? Polo? Well, now, I think I've heard of them. Was one of them a big red-bearded man with a great eye for a horse and a great eye for a woman?"

"That would be my Uncle Matthew."

"For God's sake! And was the other a cold, dark man, a good judge of a jewel and a grand judge of a sword?"

"My father, Nicholas Polo."

"For God's sake! Yoy're the son of one and the nephew of the other!"

"Did you know them?"

"Ah, laddie, how would I be knowing people like that! Sure, they're great folks high in the esteem of the grand Khan, and I'm only a poor sailorman."

"But you heard of them."

"I heard of them. They were in good health. And I heard they were on their way home, though they would travel overland and not risk the great dangers of the sea. I suppose, if they go back to China, you'll be going with them?"

"I don't know," says Macro Polo.

"You ought to see China. It's a great country, a beautiful country."

"It would have to be very great and beautiful," says Macro Polo, "to outweigh the greatness and the beauty that are here. You mustn't think I'm running down your country, mister," says he; "but for greatness, where is the beating of Venice in this day? What struck Constantinople like a thunderbolt but the mailed hand of Venice? When the Barbary corsairs roamed the seven seas, so that it was no more safe for a merchant vessel to be sailing than for a babe to be walking through a wild jungle, it was Venice who accepted the challenge and made the great sea as peaceful as the Grand Canal. Who humbled proud Genoa? And hurled the Saracen from Saint John of Acre's walls? Venice. And as for magnificence, the retinue of our doge when he goes to marry the sea with a ring it makes the court of Lorenzo seem like a huckster's train."

"It is a crowning city."

"And as for beauty, sir," went on Marco Polo, "there is nothing in the world like San Marco's, and it ablaze in the setting sun, and the great pillars before it rising in tongues of flame. And was there ever in all time anything like the Grand Canal at the dusk of day, and the torches beginning to show like fireflies, and the lap of the water, and stringed music, and the great barges going by like swans, now a battle-hacked captain of war, now a great gracious lady? And the moon does be rising . . .

"You've sailed all the way from China and seen strange and beautiful things, but I remember one summer's day, when I took out my little sailing-boat and went out on the water to compose a poem for a lady, and the water was blue—oh, as blue as the sky's self, and the sands of the Lido were silver, and the water shuffled gently over them, as gently as a child's little feet. And there was a clump of olive trees there so green as to be black, and there alighted before it a great scarlet Egyptian bird. And the beauty of that brought the tears to my eyes, so that I thought of nuns in their cells and barefoot friars in the hollow lands, and they striving for paradise. What did I care about paradise? A Venetian I. So why should I want to go to China?"

"You have made a great case for the grandeur and beauty of Venice," says the sea-captain. "It is lovely, surely," says he, filling his pipe; "but finer poets nor you, my lad," says he, lighting it, "have tried to describe the grace and beauty of Tao-Tuen, and," says he taking a draw, "have failed."

"Tao-Tuen is a beautiful name. It is like two notes plucked on a harp. And it must be a wonderful place, surely, if great poets cannot describe it."

"It is not a place," said the captain, "it's a girl."

"As for women, Venice—"

"Venice be damned!" said the sea-captain. "Not in Venice, not in all the world, is there the like for grace or beauty of Tao-Tuen. They call her Golden Bells," he says.

"Is she a dancing-girl?" Marco asked.

"She is not a dancing-girl," says the sea-captain, "she is the daughter of Kubla, the great Khan."

"A cold and beautiful princess," says Marco Polo.

"She is not a cold and beautiful princess," says the sea-captain. "She is warm as the sun in early June, and she may be beautiful and a princess, but we all think of her as Golden Bells, the little girl in the Chinese garden."

"Did you ever see her?" says Marco, eagerly. "Tell me."

"I saw her before I left," says the sea-captain. "I was at the Khan's palace of Chagannor," says he, "seeing of the chief of the stewards was there anything I could get for him, and I in foreign parts. And as I was being rowed back along the river by my ten brawny sailormen, what did I pass but the garden of Golden Bells.

"And there she was by the river-side, a little brown slip of a girl in green coat and trousers, with a flower in her dark hair.

"And I lower my head in reverence as we pass by. But I hear her low, merry voice, by reason of which they call her Golden Bells.

" 'Ho, master of the vessel!' she calls. 'Where do you go?'

"And the sailors back water with a swish, and I stand up respectfully, for all she is only a slip of a girl.

" 'I go to foreign parts, Golden Bells,' I tell her; 'to far and dangerous places, into the Indian Ocean. To the Island of Unicorns and to the land where men eat men.'

" 'I hope you come back safe, master of the vessel,' she says. 'I hope you have a good voyage and come back safe. It must be a dreadful strain on your people to think of you so far away.'

" 'In all this wide land,' I tell her, 'there is none to worry about me. I have neither chick nor child.'

" 'Golden Bells will worry about you, then,' she said, 'and you in the hazards of the sea. And take this flower for luck.' And she gave me the flower from her hair. 'And let it bring you luck against the anger of the ocean and the enemies all men have. And let me know when you are back, because I'll be worried about a man of China and him in danger on the open sea.'

"And wasn't that a wonderful thing from a daughter of Kubla to me, a poor sailor man?

"The son of the King of Siam came to woo her with a hundred princes on a hundred elephants, but she wouldn't have him. 'I don't wish to be a queen,' she told her father. 'How could I be a queen? I am only Golden Bells.' Nor would she have anything to say to the Prince of the Land of Darkness, who came to her with sea ivory and pale Arctic gold. 'The sun of China is in my heart, and you wouldn't have me go up into the great coldness to shiver and die?'

"So she remains in her garden by the lake of Cranes with Li Po, the great poet, him they call the Drinker of Wine, to make songs for her; and the *Sanang* Tung-Chih, the great magician, to perform wonders for her when she is wearied; and Bulagan, her nurse, to take her to her heart when she is sad.

"And sad she is a lot of the time, they tell me. She sits in her garden in the dusk, playing her lute, and singing the song of the Willow branches, which is the saddest love-song in the world . . .

"And why she should be singing a sad love-song, is a mystery, for her soft, brown beauty is the flower of the world. For there would be no lack of suitors for her, nor is she the one to refuse love. The only thing I make of it is that the right hour hasn't come.

"The beauty of Venice jumps to your eyes, but the beauty of this pulls at your heart. Little brown Golden Bells, in her Chinese garden, singing the song of the Willow Branches at the close of day . . . Is that not better nor Venice?"

But he got no word out of Marco Polo, sitting with his chin cupped in his hands. And that was the finest answer at all, at all . . .

V

The times went by, and Marco Polo busied himself with his daily affairs, keeping track of the galleasses with merchandise to strange far-away ports, buying presents for refractory governors who didn't care for foreign trade in their domains, getting wisdom from the old clerks, and knowledge from the mariners; in the main, acting as the son of a great house while the heads of it were away.

You would think that he would have forgotten what the sea-captain of China told him about Golden Bells, what with work and sport and other women near him. You would think that would drop out of his memory like an old rime. But it stuck there, as an old rime sometimes sticks, and by dint of thinking he had her fast now in his mind—so fast, so clear, so full of life, that she might be someone he had seen an hour ago or was going to see an hour from now. He would think of the now merry, now sad eyes of her, and the soft, sweet voice of her by reason of which they called her Golden Bells, and the dusky little face, and the hair like black silk, and the splotch of the red flower in it. She was as distinct to him as the five fingers on his hand. It wasn't only she was clear in his mind's eye, but she was inside of him, closer than his heart. She was there when the sun rose, so he would be saying, "It's a grand day is in it surely, Golden Bells." She was there in the dim counting house and he going over in the great intricate ledgers the clerks do be posting carefully with quills of the gray goose, so that he would be saying: "I wonder where this is and that is. Sure I had my finger on it only a moment ago, Golden Bells." And when the dusk was falling, and the bats came out, and the quiet of Christ was over everything, and the swallows flew low on the great canals, she would be beside him, and never a word would he say to her, so near to him would she be.

And she wrought strangeness between him and the women he knew, the great grave lady with the large, pale mouth, her that was of his mind, and the little black cloak maker with the eager, red mouth, her that was closer than mind or heart to him. So that the first found fault with his poetry.

"I don't know what's come over you, Marco Polo,"—and there was a touch of temper in her voice,—"but these poems of yours show me you haven't your mind on your subject. Would you mind telling me when I had bound black hair?" she says. "And you say my bosom is like two little russet apples. Now, a regular poet once compared it to two great silver cups, and that was a good comparison, though in truth," she says, "he knew as little about it as you. And my hands are not like soft Eastern flowers. They're like lilies. I don't know where you do be getting these Eastern comparisons," she says. "But I don't like them. Tell me, pretty boy,"— she looks suspicious,—"you haven't been taking any of the strange Egyptian drugs the dark people do be selling in the dim shops on the quiet canals? Look out, pretty boy! look out!"

And the little cloak-maker grumbled when he was gone. "I don't know what's wrong with him," says she. "Or maybe it's something that's wrong with myself, but this delicate love isn't all it's cracked up to be. It's all right in books," she says, "and it's a grand sight, and the players doing it; but I like a hug," she says, "would put the breath out of you; and a kiss," she says, "you could feel in the soles of your feet." And she lay awake and grumbled. "Let him be taking his la-di-da courting to those as favour it," says she. "It's not my kind," and she grumbled through the lonely night. "I wonder where my husband is now," she said. "And wasn't I the foolish girl to be sending him off! Sure, he drank like a fish and beat me something cruel, but he was a rare lover, and the mood on him. Sure, a woman never knows when she's well off," says she.

And Marco Polo didn't miss them any more nor you'd miss an old overcoat and the winter past. All his mind was on was the Golden Bells of China. And he thought long until his uncle and father came, so that he could be off with them to the strange Chinese land.

"But there's no use to me going there," says he. "I couldn't marry her. She would laugh at me," he says. "She, who refused the son of the King of Siam, with his hundred princes on a hundred elephants, what use would she have for me, who's no better nor a pedler with his pack? But it would be worth walking the world barefoot for to see that little golden face, to hear the low, sweet voice they call Golden Bells."

They came back in due time, his uncle Matthew, the red, hairy man, and his father, the thin, dark man, who knew precious stones. And he told them he wanted to go with them when they made their next expedition to China.

"We could be using you, after your training in trade," says the father. But Marco Polo would take no interest in barter. "Sure, you'd better come along," says his uncle Matthew. "There's great sport to be had on the road, kissing and courting the foreign women and not a word of language between you, barring a smile and a laugh."

"I have no interest in the foreign women, Uncle Matthew."

"Then it's the horses you've been hearing about, the fine Arab horses faster nor the wind, and the little Persian ponies they do be playing polo on, and the grand Tatar hunters that can jump the height of a man, and they sure-footed as a goat. Ah, the horses, the bonny horses!"

"Ah, sure, Uncle Matthew, 'tis little I know of horses. Sure, I know all about boats, racing and trade and war boats, but a horse is not kin to me."

"Then what the hell's the use of your going to China?"

"Ah, sure, that's the question I'm asking myself, Uncle Matthew. But I have to go. I do so. There is something calling me, Uncle Matthew—a bell in my ear, father's brother, and there's a ringing bell in my heart."

VI

I shall now tell you how it came about that Marco Polo went to China with his uncle and father, though he had no eye for a bargain, or interest in courting foreign women, or sense of horses.

Now, as you may know, this was a great religious time. The Crusaders, feeling shame that the Sepulchre of the Lord Jesus should be in Saracen hands, had come with horse, foot and artillery to Palestine to give tribute of arms to Him who had died for them on the Bitter Tree. And great feats were performed and grand battles won. And kings became saints, like Louis of France, and saints became kings, like Baldwin of Constantinople. Mighty wonders were seen and miracles performed so that people said, "Now will be the second coming of Christ and the end of the world."

And a great desire came on the Christian people to tell the truth of Christ to the strange and foreign peoples of the world. So that every day out of Jerusalem you would see friars hitting the road, some of them to confront the wizards of the Land of Darkness, and some to argue theology with the old lamas of Tibet, and some to convert the sunny Southern islands, where the young women do be letting down their hair and the men do be forgetting God for them. And all over the world there was spreading a great rumour that the truth of all things was at last known.

Even Kubla Khan had heard of it far off in China, and he had charged the uncle and father of Marco with a message to the Pope of Rome. Let the Pope be sending some theologians to his court, and they'd argue the matter out; and if he was satisfied that this new religion was the True Religion, then he'd turn Christian and tell his people to turn Christian, too. And let them be bringing back some of the Oil of the Lamp which burns in the Holy Sepulchre at Jerusalem and is a cure for all the ills in the world.

And when they came to the City of Acre, sure the Pope was dead. And they waited a long time, but no new Pope was chosen, so they decided to go back, because they had a good business there, and they didn't want to lose it. And yet they knew there'd be trouble with the Grand Khan, if they didn't bring back the news of the True Religion and people to argue it.

"I've been a long time trading," says Nicolo, "and it's a queer thing, but the more trading you do, the less religion you have. The arguing of religion would not come easy to me. And I'd be up against experts. I'm not the man for it," says he. "How about you, Matthew?"

"Oh, sure, they'd never listen to me," Matthew laughs—"me that's drank with them, and deludhered their women, and gambled until I left them nothing but the sweat of their brows. I'd be a great one to preach religion to them. Why, man, they'd laugh at me. But I tell you what, Nicolas. There's a bishop in Negropont, and I know where he lives, and I know his house and everything. What do you say, Nicolas? We'll just throw a bag over his head and tie him on a horse. Oh, sure, he'd give grand discourses to the Great Khan!"

"Have sense, Matthew; have sense. You're always too rough; always ready to end an argument with a knife, or just lift what you want. Have sense, man; you can't kidnap a bishop like you'd kidnap a woman."

"Well, I don't see why not," says Matthew. "It would be easier, too, because a woman will scratch like a wildcat. But if you're set against it, I won't do it," he says. "Well, then, how about young Marco?"

"My sound man Matthew! my bully fellow! Sure you were never at a loss yet! Young Marco it is; sure, 'tis the elegant idea. There's not a man born of woman better for the job."

Now, all the Christian world had gone religious, and young Marco was no exception; for 'tis not only the old that are religious. The young are, too; but there's a difference. The religion of old men is reason and translation; the religion of the young is just a burning cloud. The Tragedy of the Bitter Tree is not a symbol to them, but a reality, and their tears are not of the spirit, but of the body, too.

And there are no half-way houses, no compromises, in a young man's creed. It's swallow all, or be damned to you. It's believe or be lost.

And thinking over the little girl in the Chinese garden, there had come into Marco's heart a thought past enduring. If little Golden Bells did not believe, then little Golden Bells was lost. She might have everything in this world, in this life, an emperor for a father, kings for suitors, a great poet for a minstrel, a wizard for an entertainer; but once the little blue shadow left her body, she was lost forever. And the sight came to him of little Golden Bells going down the dim and lonely alleys of death, and weeping, weeping, weeping . . . Her eyes would be shot with panic, and the little mouth twisted, and the little flowery hands twitching at each other. And it would be cold there for her who was so warm, and it would be dark there for her who loved light, and the Golden Bells of her voice would be lost in the whistling and clanging of the stars as they swung by in their orbits. He to be in the great delight of paradise, and she to be in the blue-gray maze between the worlds—what tragedy!

Kings might bring her presents, a husband might bring her happiness; but if he could only bring her salvation! If he could only tell her of the Bitter Tree!

The body, when you came to think of it, mattered little. All the beauty in the world could not endure more than its appointed span. Helen was dust now, and Deirdre nothing. What had become of the beauty of Semiramis, Alexander's darling; and Cleopatra, who loved the great proconsul; and Bathsheba, for whom David of the Psalms fell from grace? And Balkis, queen of Sheba, with her apes, ivory, and peacocks? Dust and ashes, dust and ashes! And Scheherazade was but a strange, sad sound. Beauty increased and waned like the moon. A little shadow around the eyes, a little crinkle in the neck, the backs of the hands stiffening like parchment. Dust and ashes, dust and ashes!

But the little blue shadow would glow like an Easter morning.

Or it would be a poor, lonely, unlit shadow in the cold gloom of the clanging worlds.

Poor Golden Bells! Poor little weeping Golden Bells! If he could only tell her about the Bitter Tree!

And then what happens but his uncle Matthew claps him on the back.

"How would you like to go to China, Marco Markeen," says he, "and preach religion to the benighted people!"

"How did you know, Uncle Matthew?"

"How did I know what?"

"That I wanted to go to China and preach religion to the—the people!"

"Well, if that doesn't beat Banagher," says Matthew Polo, "and Banagher beats the devil! Tell me, did you ever hear an old tune called 'Bundle and Go!'?"

And so the three of them leave upon their journey, but at Layas, where the King of Armenia had his castle, they heard of the election of a new Pope, so they came back to Acre to get his instructions and blessing.

VII

The Pope said a grand mass for them, and at the gospel he enters the pulpit, a burly figure of a man with sad eyes.

"The blessing of the Father and the Son and the Holy Ghost be with you and about you, Amen.

"It is not to you, Nicolo Polo, that I wish to speak, nor to you, Matthew Polo, for neither of you are my ambassadors to the Great Khan. Merchant and sportsman, I honor you, and you have my blessing, but you have no hopes of mine. The dirty diversions of the world are between your eyes and glory," said he. "It's only myself, an old and sorrowful man, and this child, a young and hopeful one, can understand; old men having sight of visions, and young men dreaming dreams . . .

"Now in the matter of converting the Great Khan and his numerous millions, first let wisdom speak. I have little hopes. He wants to be argued into it, you see. Religion is not a matter of argument. It is a wisdom that surpasses wisdom. It drifts in men's souls as the foggy dew comes unbidden to the trees. It is born before our soul, as the horned moon is born before our eyes.

"And now, my child, you might say, 'What is the use of sending me to China if he knows I cannot bring these millions into the fold?' My dear son, there is the wisdom surpassing wisdom. A great and noble thought must not die. Things of the spirit we cannot reckon as a husbandman reckons his crops. There is a folk on the marches of Europe, and they are ever going into battle, and they always fall. Their results are nothing. But their name and their glory will endure forever . . .

"My dear son, God has put wisdom in my head and beauty into yours. Wisdom is needed for the governance of this world, but beauty is needed for its existence. In arid deserts there is no life. Birds do not sing in the dark of night. Show me a waste country, and I'll show you a brutal people. No faith can live that is not beautiful . . .

"The beauty God has put in your heart, child, you must always keep . . . How much I think of it I'll tell you. I'm an old man now, an old and broken man, and in a few years I'll stand before my Master.

" 'What have you seen on my earth,' He'll ask me, 'you who followed St. Peter!'

" 'Lord! Lord!' I'll tell Him, 'I've seen mighty things. I've seen the bridegroom leave his bride and the king his kingdom, the huckster leave his booth, and the reaper drop his hook, that they might rescue Your Holy Sepulchre from pagan hands.'

" 'And anything else?' He'll ask.

" 'And I've seen a young man go out into the desert and over his head was a star . . .'

"You may think you have failed, child, but remember that in the coming times your name and fame will awaken beauty, and many's the traveller on the hard road will find his courage again, and he thinking of Marco Polo. And many's the young man will dream dreams, and many 's the old man will see visions, and they reading the book by the golden candlelight; and many's the young girl will give you love, and you dead for centuries. But for this you must keep your dream.

"Now you'll think it's the queer Pope I am to be telling you things like this instead of demanding converts. But the wisdom that surpasses wisdom comes to you with the Anointing of the Oil. 'I knew a man in Christ above fourteen years ago,' writes Saint Paul, '(whether in the body I cannot tell, or whether out of the body I cannot tell. God knoweth.)'

" 'How that he was caught up into paradise, and heard unspeakable words, which is not lawful for a man to utter.'

"Now you see there is a wisdom surpassing wisdom, and it is out of this fount of wisdom I am drawing when I speak to you these words.

"Child, I will not keep you any longer. Only to say this, and this is the chiefest thing: never let your dream be taken from you. Keep it unspotted from the world. In darkness and in tribulation it will go with you as a friend; but in wealth and power hold fast to it, for then is danger. Let not the mists of the world, the gay diversions, the little trifles, draw you from glory.

"Remember!

"*Si oblitus fuero tui Jerusalem,*—If I forget thee, O Jerusalem,—

"*Oblivioni detur dextera mea,*—let my right hand forget her cunning—

"*Adhaereat lingua mea faucibus tnels, si non meminero tui,*—if I do not remember thee, let my tongue cleave to the roof of my mouth—

"*Si non proposuero Jerusalem, in principis laetit'ue meae,*—if I prefer not Jerusalem above my chief joy.

"I shall now send a prayer to Heaven," he said, "to keep you safe in the strange foreign ways, to protect you against wind and tempest, against pestilence and sudden death, against the powers of darkness, and Him who goes up and down the world for the ruin of souls."

And he turned to the high altar again, and now you'd hear his voice loud and powerful, and now low and secret, and the bell struck, and the acolyte intoned the responses, and all of a sudden he turned and spread forth his hands.

"*Ite*! Let you go now. *Miss a est.*"

VIII

And so they set forth with their great train of red, snarling camels and little patient donkeys and slender, nervous horses toward the rising sun. Behind them the green hills of Palestine died out as a rainbow dies out, and now there was sand before them and now bleak mountains, and by day the wind was swift and hot and by night it was black and cold. And moons were born and died . . .

And they passed through the land of the King of Armenia, and they passed Ararat, the mountain where Noë brought his ark to anchor, and where it still is, and where it can be seen still, but cannot be reached, so cold and high and terrible is that mountain.

And they passed ruined Babel, that was built of Nimrod, the first king of the world, and now is desolation. They passed it on a waning moon. And out of the ruins the dragons came and hissed at them, and strange, obscene birds flapped their wings in the air and cawed and pecked at them, and over the desert the satyr called unto her mate . . .

And they passed through the Kingdom of Georgia, whose kings are born with the mark of an eagle on their right shoulder. They passed through Persia, where the magicians worship fire. And they passed through the city of Saba, where sleep the three magi who came to worship at Bethlehem, and their names were Kaspar, Balthasar, and Melchior.

And they passed through Camadi, where great ruins are and robbers roam through the magical darkness. And they passed northward of the Perilous Valley, where the Devil's Head is in black stone, and that is one of the nine entrances to hell; and passed the Valley of the Cockadrills, where there are serpents five fathoms in length; and passed the Valley of Cruel Women, who have precious stones in place of eyes . . .

And they went through the Dismal Desert, where no stream sang . . .

And in the desert they passed the Trees of the Sun and Moon, which speak with the voices of men. And it was from the Speaking Tree that Alexander heard of his death. And it was near there that he and Darius fought. And they passed the *Arbre Sec*, the Dry Tree, which has a green bark on one side and white on the other, and there are no trees within a hundred miles of that tree, and it is sprung from the staff of Adam.

And they passed through Balkh, the Mother of Cities. And they passed through Taihan, where the great salt mountains are. And they passed through Badashan, where the mountains of the rubies are. And they passed through Kashmir, whose women are very beautiful, and whose magicians weave the strongest spells in the world . . .

And moons were born and died . . .

And they came to Alamoot, the fortress of *Senex de Monte*, the Old Man of the Mountain, the King of the Assassins, the greatest wizard of all time . . .

Now this is the tale of the Old Man of the Mountain.

Whenever within his dominions there was a fine young horseman, the Old Man would put a spell on him and draw him to the Castle of Alamoot, and outside of the castle sleep would come on him. And when he woke up, he would be inside the castle, in the wonderful gardens. And they'd tell him he was dead and in paradise. And paradise it would be for him, what with the lovely women and the great playing on the flutes, the birds singing, and the sun shining, the crystal rivers and the flowers of the world. And after a while the Old Man of the Mountain would call for him, and tell him he was sending him back on earth again on a mission to punish Such-and-Such. And the Old Man would put sleep on him and a knife in his hand, and when he woke he would be outside the Castle of Alamoot. And he would start on his mission. And when he came back he would be readmitted to paradise. And if he didn't come back, there were others to take his place.

The Old Man of the Mountain always kept one hundred and one assassins and four hundred and four women to tend them.

Now when the caravan of the Polos had come to rest for the day, the Old Man of the Mountain put out white, not black magic, and he drew Marco Polo to the castle as a magnet draws a needle. And Marco Polo galloped up to the Castle in the waning moon, and the Old Man looked down on him from the battlements and stroked his long white beard.

"Do you know me, Marco Polo?"

"I know you and I have no fear of you, Old Man of the Mountain."

"And why have you no fear of me, Marco Polo?"

"Because the cross of the Lord Jesus is between me and harm. Because it protects me night and day."

"I know Eesa ben-Miriam," said the Old Man. "He was a great prophet. But whether he would have protected you from me, we will differ about that. I've often thought of you, Marco Polo, and you coming this way. I could have used you in my work of keeping the kings and chieftains of the world in fear and subjection."

"Then why amn't I in your garden, Old Man of the Mountain?"

"The four most beautiful women in the world are in my garden. There is a tall, black-haired woman, and she is fairer and more adroit than Lilith, who was before Eve; and there is a tall, blonde woman, and she is like a queen; and there is a slim, copper-coloured woman, and she is like an idol in a shrine; and there is a little brown-haired woman, and she is like a child. But none of those women could make you believe you were in paradise while there's a face in your heart. Not the cross of the Lord Jesus is between you and me, but the face of little Golden Bells of China."

"But I am not going to China to woo Golden Bells, Old Man of the Mountain. I am going to convert the men of Cathay."

The Old Man of the Mountain laughed and stroked his beard.

"You had a sermon from Gregory be-before you came away. Did he tell you you were to convert the men of Cathay?"

"He did not."

"Ah, Gregory's a sound man. He knew you can't make saints in a day. Why, child, I've seen the beginning of the world, and I've seen the end of it. I've seen the beginning in a crystal glass, and I've seen the end in a pool of ink in a slave's hand. I've seen mankind begin lower nor the gibbering ape, and I've seen them end the shining sons of God. Millions on millions on millions of years, multiplied unto dizziness, crawling, infinitesimal work overcoming nature, overcoming themselves, overcoming the princes of the powers of darkness, one of whom I am. But this is too deep for you, Marco Polo.

"Now you can go on your way without hindrance from me, Marco Polo, because of the memory of an old time, when the courting of a woman was more to me than the killing of a man, when beauty meant more nor power.

"Let you be on your way, Marco Polo, while I sit here a lonely old man, with wee soft ghosts whispering to him. Let you be hastening on your way before I remember I am a prince of the powers of darkness and should do you harm . . ."

IX

And so they went on eastward, ever eastward, and the moons were born, grew, waned, and died . . .

They passed through Khotan, where the divers bring up jade from the rivers, white jade and black jade, and green jade veined with gold. They passed through Carnal, the shameful city, whose women are fair and wanton, whose men are cuckolds. And they passed through the province of Chitingolos, where are the mountains of the Salamanders. They passed through the city of Campicha, where there are more idols than men. And they passed through the great city of Samarkand, where the Green Stone is on which Timur's throne was set . . . And moons were born and died . . .

They passed through Tangut, where the men will not carry the dead out through the door of a house, but must break a hole in the wall. And they passed through Kialehta, where there are snow white camels. And they passed through the lands of Prester John.

And now they were in the Tatar lands. There passed them lowing musk oxen. There passed them the wild asses of Mongolia. There passed them the barbarians, with their great tents on wheels. There passed them the black-jowled, savage idolaters. There passed them the pretty white-faced women. There passed them huge, abominable dogs.

And they came to the town of Lob, and a new moon arose, and they entered the Desert of the Singing Sands.

X

Wherever they went now was sand, and a dull haze that made the sun look like a copper coin. And a great silence fell on the caravan, and nothing was heard but the crunch of the camels' pads and the tinkle of the camels' bells. And no green thing was seen.

And a great terror fell on the caravan, so that one night a third of the caravan deserted. The rest went on in silence under the dull sun. And now they came across a village of white skeletons grinning in the silent sand. And at night there was nothing heard, not even the barking of a dog. And others of the caravan deserted, and others were lost.

And now they had come so far into the desert that they could not return, but must keep on their way, and on the fifth day they came to the Hill of the Drum. And all through the night they could not sleep for the booming of the Drum. And some of the caravan went mad there, and fled screaming into the waste.

And now there was only a great haze about them, and they looked at one another with terror, saying: "Were we ever any place where green was, where birds sang, or there was sweet water? Or maybe we are dead. Or maybe this was all our life, and the pleasant towns, and the lamplight in the villages, and the apricots in the garden, and our wives and children, maybe they were all a dream that we woke in the middle of. Let us lie down and sleep that we may dream again."

But Marco Polo would not let them lie down, for to lie down was death. But he drove them onward. And again they complained: "Surely God never saw this place that He left it so terrible. Surely He was never here. He was never here."

And now that their minds were pitched to the height of madness, the warlocks of the desert took shape and jeered at them, and the white-sheeted ghosts flitted alongside of them, and the goblins of the Gobi harried them from behind. And the sun was like dull copper through the haze, and the moon like a guttering candle, and stars there were none.

And when the moon was at its full, they came to the Hill of the Bell. And through the night the Bell went *gongh, gongh, gongh,* until they could feel it in every fibre of their bodies, and their skin itched with it. They would stop their ears. But they would hear it in the palms of their hands and the soles of their feet. *Gongh, gongh, gongh.*

And when they left the Hill of the Bell there were only six of the caravan left, and a multitude of white-sheeted ghosts. And the caravan plodded onward dully. And now the warlocks of the desert played another cruelty. Afar off they would put a seeming of a lake, and the travellers would press on gladly, crying, "There is water! water! God lives! God lives!" But there was only sand. And now it would be a green vision, and they would cry: "We have come to the edge of the desert. After the long night, dawn. God lives! God lives!" But there would be only sand, sand. And now it would be a city of shining domes in the distance. And they would nudge one another and croak, "There are men there, brother, secure streets, and merchants in their booths; people to talk with, and water for our poor throats." But there would be only sand, sand, sand ... And they would cry like children. "God is dead! Haven't you heard? Don't you know? God is dead in His heaven, and the warlocks are loosed on the land!"

And on the last day of the moon they were all but in sight of the desert's edge, though they didn't know. And the goblins and the warlocks took counsel, for they were now afraid Marco and his few people would escape. They gathered together and they read the runes of the Flowing Sand.

And suddenly the camels rushed screaming into the desert with sudden panic, and a burning wind came, and the sands rose, and the desert heeled like a ship, and the day became night.

And young Marco Polo could stand no more. That was the end, the end of him, the end of the world, the end of everything. There was red darkness everywhere, and he could see nobody. "O my Lord Jesus!" he cried. "O little Golden Bells!" The wind boomed like an organ. The sand screamed. "O my Lord Jesus! O little Golden Bells!" And the voices of his father and uncle were like the tweeting birds. "Where's the lad, Matthew? Where's our lad?" "Mark, Mark, where have you got to? Lad of our heart, where are you?" But they couldn't find each other. The sand buffeted them like shuttlecocks. "Boy Mark!" The sand snarled like a dog; the wind hammered like drums. "Oh, Golden Bells! O, little Golden Bells! O, my Lord Jesus, must it end here?"

And the fight went out of him, and a big sob broke in him, and he lay down to die . . .

XI

I shall now tell you of Golden Bells, and her in the Chinese Garden.

XII

I would have you now see her as I see her, standing before Li Po, the great poet, in her green costume. And Li Po, big, fat, with sad eyes and a twisted mouth, uncomfortable as be damned. The sun shone in the garden, the butterflies, the red and black and golden butterflies, flitted from blossom to blossom. And the bees droned. And on the banks of the green lake the kingfisher tunnelled his wee house, and the wind shook the blossoms of the apple-trees. And Li Po sat on the marble slab and was very uncomfortable. And in a dark bower was *Sanang*, the magician, brooding like an owl. And Golden Bells stood before Li Po, and there were hurt tears in her eyes.

"Did my father or I ever do anything to you, Li Po, that you should make a song such as they sing in the marketplace?"

"What song?"

"The Song of the Cockatoo."

"I don't remember."

"I'll remind you, Li Po. 'There alighted on the balcony of the King of Annam,' the song goes, 'a red cockatoo. It was coloured as a peach-tree blossom and it spoke the tongue of men. And the King of Annam did to it what is always done to the learned and eloquent. He took a cage with stout bars, and shut it up inside.' And wasn't that the cruel thing to write! And are you so imprisoned here, Li Po? Ah, Li Po, I'm thinking hard of you, I'm thinking hard."

"Well, now, Golden Bells, to tell you the truth there was no excuse for it. But often times I do be feeling sad, and thinking of the friends of my youth who are gone. Yuan Chen, who might have been a better poet nor me, if he had been spared; and H'sieng-yang and Li Chien, too. Ah, they were great poets, Golden Bells. They never sang a poor song, Golden Bells, that they might wear a fine coat. And they'd write what was true, wee mistress, were all the world to turn from them. And I'm the laureate now, the court singer, living in my glory, and they're dead with their dreams. I'm the last of the seven minstrels. And, wee Golden Bells, I do be thinking long.

"And sometimes an old woman in the street or a man with gray in his hair will lift a song, and before the words come to me, there's a pain in my heart.

"And I go down to the drinking booths, and the passion of drinking comes on me—a fury against myself and a fury against the world. And the folk do be following me to see will I let drop one gem of verse that they can tell their grandchildren they heard from the lips of Li Po. And when my heart is high with the drinking, I take a lute from a travelling poet, and not knowing what I'm saying, I compose the song. Out of fallow sorrow bloom the little songs. You mustn't be hard on an old man, wee Golden Bells, and he thinking long for his dead friends."

"Ah, poor Li Po," she said, and she had grown all soft again. "Is it so terrible to be old?"

"Now you ask me a question, Golden Bells, and I'll give you an answer. Besides, it's part of my duties to teach you wisdom. Now, it is not a terrible thing, at all, at all, to be old. I see the young folk start out in life, and before them there's the showers of April, there's wind and heat and thunder and lightning. But I'm in warm, brown October, and all of it's gone by me. And in a little while I'll sleep, and 'tis I need it, God help me! The old don't sleep much, wee Golden Bells, so 'tis a comfort to look forward to one's rest after the hardness of the world. In a hundred or more years or five hundred, just as the fancy takes me, I'll wake up for a while and wander down the world to hear the people sing my songs, and then I'll go back to my sleep."

And she was going to ask him another question when the *Sanang* came up. The magician was a thick man with merry eyes and a cruel mouth.

"Golden Bells," he says, "there's rare entertainment in the crystal glass."

"What is it, *Sanang*?"

"The warlocks of the Gobi have a young lad down, and they're waiting until the soul comes out of his body. Come, I'll show you."

And in the crystal glass he showed her Marco Polo, and the knees going from under him in the roaring sands. She gave a quick cry of pity.

"Oh, the poor lad!"

Sanang chuckled. "He started out with a big caravan to preach what he thought was a truth to China. I've been watching him all along, and it's been rare sport. I knew it would come to this."

"Couldn't you save him, *Sanang*?" she cried. "O, *Sanang*, he's so young, and he set out to come to us. Couldn't you save him?"

"Well, I might." *Sanang* was not pleased. "It'll be a while before the shadow comes out of him. But it would be rare sport to watch and see the warlocks and the ghouls and the goblins set on it the way terriers do be setting on an otter."

"Oh, save him, *Sanang*! Save him!"

"Now, Golden Bells, I might be able to save him, and again I mightn't."

"Save him, *Sanang*!" Li Po broke in. "Save him the way the wee one wants. For if you don't, *Sanang*, I'll write a song about you that'll be remembered for generations, and they'll point out your grandchildren and your grandchildren's grandchildren, and they'll laugh and sing Li Po's song:

" 'There was a fat worm who considered himself a serpent—' "

"Oh, now, Li Po, for God's sake, let you not be composing poems on me, for 'tis you have the bitter tongue. Promise me now, and I'll save him. We'll send for the keeper of the Khan's drums."

And they sent for the keeper, and *Sanang* gave a message to be put on the Speaking Drums.

"Let you now," he told his helper, "get me the Distant Ears."

And the helper brought him the Golden Ears, which were the like of a great bird's wings, and he put them on his head and he listened.

"I hear the drums of the battlements," he said, ". . . and I hear the Drums of the Hill of Graves . . ."

And he listened a while, and Golden Bells was white.

"I hear the Drums of the Dim Mountain," . . . and for a while he said nothing.

"Those would be the drums of Yung Chang . . ."

"I hear the Drums of Kai Yu Kwan," he said.

"Yes, *Sanang*, yes." Little Golden Bells was one quiver of fear.

"I hear the Drums of the Convent of the Red Monks," said *Sanang*. "I hear drums calling the Tatar tribes . . . I hear the slap of saddles. I hear the jingle of bits . . . I hear galloping ponies . . .

"Yes, *Sanang*. Oh, hurry, *Sanang*! hurry!"

He listened a little while longer, and then he took off the Distant Ears.

"Your man's saved," he said.

Then little Golden Bells laughed and then she cried. She caught Li Po's hand and laughed again and again she cried. *Sanang* shook his head to get out of his ears the deafening noises of the world. And Li Po smiled out of his sad eyes.

"I think I'll go and write a marriage song, Golden Bells."

"Whom will you write the marriage song for, Li Po?"

"I'll write it for you, Golden Bells."

"But I'm not going to be married, Li Po. There is no-one. I love no-one, Li Po. I do not. I do not, indeed."

"Then take your lute and sing me the 'Song of the Willow Branches,' which is the saddest song in the world."

She shook her head, and blushed. "I cannot sing that song, Li Po. I don't feel like singing that song."

"Then I must write you another song, Little Golden Bells . . ."

XIII

And now when Marco Polo was rested and had recovered, they brought him from the Convent of the Red Monks to where the Khan was in the city of Chandu. Now, there were two palaces in Chandu; there was the winter palace, which was of marble, and the summer palace, which was of gilt cane. Around these palaces there was built a wall sixteen miles in compass, and inside of it was a park of fountains, and rivers and brooks with the speckled trout in them, and meadows with the lark at her ease in the grass, and trees of all varieties where the little birds do be building and none to grudge them a home. And all the wild animals were abundant, the timid hare and the wild deer and the wee croaking frogs, long-legged colts by their white mothers, and little dogs tumbling over themselves with the sport of spring. Brown bees among the clover, strawberries in profusion, trees would delight your eyes, and brown cows and black cows, and dappled moilies under the great leaves of them, and lambs would be snowy of fleece. All the flowers of the world were there; the paradise of wild things it was, the park of Kubla Khan.

"In Xanadu did Kubla Khan," quoted young Randall,
     "A stately pleasure dome decree,
Where Alph, the sacred river, ran
Through caverns measureless to man,
     Down to a sunless sea.
So twice five miles of fertile ground
With walls and towers were girdled round:
And there were gardens, bright with sinuous rills,

Where blossomed many an incense-bearing tree;
And here were forests ancient as the hills,
   Enfolding sunny spots of greenery."

"Whose poem is that poem, Brian Oge?"

"It is a poem of Coleridge's, Malachi."

"I thought it was maybe a poem of Colquitto Dall McCracken of Skye, that one of you lads had put English on. It is a poem of the head, you ken, and Coloquitto, being a dark man, could only see with the eye's ghost. But it hasn't the warmth, the life of the work of Blind Coloquitto. Brain Oge, do you mind the poem Angus More Campbell of Rathlin wrote to Colquitto Dall?"

" '*Is aoibhinn duid, Colquitto Dall,*' " I remembered: "It is happy for thee, blind Colquitto, who dost not see much of women. If thou wert to see what we see, thou wouldst be tormented even as I am. My sorrow, O God, that I was not stricken blind before I saw her amber, twisted hari!"

"That's it, that's it, Brain Oge. But this is not the place to be talking of poetry. There is no poetry in this story.

"I will now tell you of Marco Polo and him entering the presence of the great Khan . . ."

XIV

And Marco Polo was brought into the presence. And among all assembled there you could hear a pin drop.

At the north end of the great hall sat the Khan himself, and Marco Polo nearly dropped with surprise; for where he expected a great, magnificent figure of a man, with majesty shining from his eyes, he saw only a pleasant, bearded man, not quarter so well dressed as the meanest servant on the room, and a fine, welcoming smile in his face. His throne was elevated so that his feet were on the level of the heads of the kinsmen of the Blood Royal beneath him, and they in silk and ermine and fine brocades and jewels. And beneath these were the barons and dukes and knights. And beneath these were the captains of the fighting men, three thousand and three. And beneath these were the musicians and the sorcerers. And behind Kubla Khan, very big, very erect, stood his three great servants, the Keeper of the Hunting Leopards, the Keeper of the Speaking Drums, and the Keeper of the Khan's Swords.

And beside Kubla Khan, on a little throne, sat Golden Bells . . . And it was the sight of her more than the sight of the great assembly that dumbed the words in his mouth. And Kubla was smiling at him, and she was smiling, too.

And Kubla saw there was something wrong with him, that there was embarrassment on him, and he rose from his throne.

"There is welcome for you here, Marco Polo, and no enmity. There is interest in and eagerness for your message. There is none here will criticise you or make it hard for you. Let there be no shame on you in speaking before so many people. Say what you have to say as if there were nobody here, if that will help you, barring myself and the little daughter beside me . . ."

"O Emperor," the words came back to Marco Polo, "and ye, great princes, dukes, and marquises, counts, knights, and burgesses, and people of all degrees who desire the light of the world, grace be to you and peace, from God our Father, and from the Lord Jesus Christ!

"The message I have to give you, I shall give in the words of Him, whose perfect message it is:

" *'Beati pauperes spiritu,*—Blessed are the poor in spirit.

" *'Quoniam ipsorum est regnum caelorum,*—For theirs is the kingdom of heaven.

" *'Beati mites,* — Blessed are the meek. . .' "

And Marco Polo went on and quoted for them the words that were spoken on the Mount in Galilee. And they listened to him with great civility and attention. And little Golden Bells leaned forward, with her chin on her hands, and Kubla leaned back in his throne, with his eyes half closed.

" 'But I say unto you, that ye resist not evil, but whoever shall smite thee on the right cheek, turn to him the other also.' " And at this the great Khan looked up puzzled, and a movement went through the fighting men in the hall. But wee Golden Bells never budged a minute, and Marco Polo went on:

" *'Et factum est; cum consummasset Jesus verba haec,*—And it came to pass when Jesus had ended these sayings, the people were astonished at his doctrine.'

"I shall now tell you of the life and death of the Lord Jesus . . ."

He told them of the birth in Bethlehem, and of the teaching on the hills, and the poets nodded their heads; and he told them of the cleansing of the lepers and of the casting out of devils and the raising of Lazarus from the dead, and the magicians wondered; and he told them of the betrayal by Judas with a kiss, and the captains-at-arms shuffled in their seats; and he told them of the scourging, and of the crowning with thorns, and the great Khan snicked his dagger in and out of the sheath. And a mist of tears came into the eyes of Golden Bells.

And he told them of the crucifixion between two thieves, and a great oath ripped from the beard of Kubla Khan, and the silver tears ran from the eyes of Golden Bells.

" 'And on the third day He arose from the dead . . .' "

And a great shout came from the throat of Kubla Khan, and he stood up.

"He arose from among the dead men, I'll warrant; He showed himself to the Roman Pilate in all His power and majesty—"

"No," said Marco Polo.

"Then He showed himself to the thousands who had seen him die upon the gallows tree!"

"No," said Marco Polo.

"Who saw Him, then?"

"His twelve Apostles and they in a little room!"

And Kubla Khan sat down suddenly and said no more. There was a moment's murmur of wonder among the assembly, and then silence. And Marco's heart fell. And he was aware of two things, of the great politeness of the Chinese people and of Golden Bell's pitying eyes . . .

XV

When Kubla Khan dismissed the assembly, and he took Marco Polo into a sitting-room, and Golden Bells came with them.

"And what did you think, sir, of what I said? And can you not see, sir, the truth that's in me?"

"Well, now, laddie," said the great Khan, "when we come to examine this sermon you quoted to us, what is there in it but the rule of the righteous man? We've had a great thinker and pious man of our own, Confucius. I'm not a reading man," says he, "but I've got an idea," says he, "that there isn't a thing you said but is embraced in the Analects. And if it isn't it'll be in the teachings of the Lord Buddha."

"Ah, but, sir," Marco Polo said, "you'll have to admit that He of whom I speak was the true God made man."

"Now, laddie, remember I'm an old man, set in my head and my ways, and I've been used to one belief so long it would be hard changing. So don't press me now; don't press me, I ask you."

"Ah, sir," pleaded Marco Polo, "it's terrible to think of as great a prince as you to be in the black spaces outside of heaven because you wouldn't accept the truth."

"Well, maybe they won't be so hard on one, my dear lad. When my time comes and I rap on the gate of your heaven, maybe they'll say: 'It's only old Kubla, the soldier, is in it. He knows devil and all about religion, but his fights were fair fights, and he never hit a man when he was down. He had a soft heart for wee children and he was easy on horses. Sure, what's the difference?

Let him in!' And if they say no, I'll tuck the old nicked claymore under my arm, and be off to where the other old fighters are."

"I see, sir, that there was little success to my message."

"I wouldn't say that," said Kubla Khan. "Wait a little until you perform miracles before the people to prove your truth. You'll know better then."

"Ah, sir," said Marco Polo, "I can perform no miracles. 'Tis only a saint can perform miracles, and I couldn't lace a saint's shoes. I have no miracles."

"Oh, well, now, my dear boy," said Kubla Khan, "I hate to tell you, but there's no use going further. Sure you'd be up against the sorcerers of the world. They'd ask you for a sign, and you'd have no sign, and they'd have signs in abundance. I wouldn't think of letting you go against them. Fair play's a jewel, and you wouldn't have a chance. There's the Red Pope from Tibet and there's the Black Magician from Korea and a hundred minor ones, and the Warlock of the North, from the Islands of Ice, who governs the hail and the snow. Child, I wouldn't let you get into the same ring with them. They'd ruin you."

"But, sir, wasn't it a great miracle of the Lord's, my rescue in the Gobi Desert?"

"A miracle of the Lord's! A miracle of Golden Bells here. It was her magician saw you, and she had the message put on the drums, and the desert patrols went to seek you. It was herself here, wee Golden Bells." And Golden Bells' mouth gave a smile of shame that his thought should be broken in his mind.

"A long way I'm after coming," said Marco Polo, "and when I set out my heart was high."

"Now, don't be taking it too hard," says the Khan, kindly. "Sure, there's a power of good you can be doing here. Maybe you can do something with Li Po," says he. "I'd like fine for you to try. The man is worrying the life out of me with his drinking. I never know when he goes out whether he'll come back all right or feet foremost on a door. For he's got the bitter tongue when the drink's in him, and China could ill afford to lose him. And there are some of my captains, and the tune they're always piping is 'War! War! War! And let's show up this Alexander who said he conquered the world.' And I'm past the age when you make war for devilment. So let you be helping me out with them, Marco Polo."

But Marco Polo knew this was only meant in kindness, and his heart was broken.

"Ah, wee lady,"—he turned to Golden Bells,—"wee lady, wee lady, why didn't you let me die in the desert? Why didn't I die?"

"And why should you die, Marco Polo?" Her low, sweet voice rang in the heart of him. "Didn't you come here to give your message? And to make converts? And didn't I hear your message? And amn't I your convert, Marco Polo?"

XVI

And now the place of Li Po was usurped, and gone *Sanang* with his magic glass, and in the jasmine garden by the Lake of Cranes Marco Polo sat and instructed Golden Bells . . .

XVII

And he told of the flight into Egypt when savage Herod reigned, and of the Jewish maid and her child sleeping beneath the shadow of the great Sphinx, while the shades of the old Afric gods looked on in reverence, Amenalk and Thoth and the moon-horned Io, Isis, and Osiris. And the painted kings knelt in their pyramids, and out of the sluggish Nile came the strange aquatic population, the torpid crocodiles and monstrous water lizards, and the great hippopotami lumbered to bow before the little Lord of all things . . .

And he told her how Satan had tempted Him on the lonely, black craigs . . .

"But you are not listening, little Golden Bells—"

"Indeed I am listening, Marco Polo. Yes, indeed I am. I love to hear your voice, Marco Polo. You are so earnest, Marco Polo; there is such a light in your eyes. Listen, Marco Polo, Li Po once wrote a poem, 'White Gleam the Gulls,' and it is the poem by which he is best known, and every time I hear it there is an echo in my heart. But, Marco Polo, I never listened to Li Po's song so eagerly as I am listening to your voice."

"But you are not taking it in, little Golden Bells."

"It is very hard to take in. Marco Polo, it happened so long ago. It is hard to think of a tragedy in a strange country, and we in this garden on the second moon of spring. And it was so very long ago. Do you hear the bees, Marco Polo—the bees among the almond blossoms? And see the blue heron by the lotus flowers? And do you see the little tortoise, Marco Polo, and he sunning himself on a leaf? If I throw a pebble, Marco Polo, he will dive, and he is such a clumsy diver, Marco Polo!"

"But you must listen, Golden Bells, and believe me."

"I do believe, Marco Polo; I honestly do. Don't you know I believe you? Anything you say, Marco Polo I believe. You wouldn't be coming all the way over the world to be telling me a lie. Of course I believe."

"And doesn't it make you happy, Golden Bells?"

"Once I was unhappy, Marco Polo. I used sit here, and on my lute I used play the 'Song of the Willow Branches,' which is the saddest song in the world. Under the moon I used be lonely, and the droning of the bees meant nothing to me, and now it is a sweet brave song. I cannot play 'Willow Branches' any more, so alien is sadness to me. And the moon smiles. I am very happy, Marco Polo."

"It is the True Religion, little Golden Bells, that makes you happy."

"Is it, Marco Polo? Is it? It must be, I suppose. I don't know what it is, but I am very happy."

XVIII

And he told her of Paul, who had seen a vision and gone preaching through the world, who was persecuted, who was shipwrecked, who was bitten by a viper, and who survived everything that he might preach the Lord Jesus. He was a fierce, ragged man with burning eyes . . . And he told her of Paul's instructions to women . . .

"You do not look at me when you speak, Marco Polo. Only your voice comes to me, not your eyes. Is it because of Paul?"

And Marco Polo felt great trouble on him, because he could not explain. But Golden Bells went on:

"There is little in your faith about women, Marco Polo. Is it a faith only for men, then? Is it against women? Must the young men not look at the young women?"

"No, Golden Bells; the young men must not look too much on the young women."

"But that is very foolish, Marco Polo. Is it wrong to see the beauty of the almond blossoms, wrong to taste the scented wind? Is it wrong to watch the kingfisher seeking his nest? Is it wrong to watch the moon, the stars? All these are very beautiful, Marco Polo, so beautiful as to make me cry. Is it wrong to watch them?"

"It is not wrong, Golden Bells. The glory of God is in the beauty of his handicraft."

"Li Po is old and wise and a great poet, Marco Polo, and Li Po says there is beauty in a running horse and beauty in a running stream; but there is no beauty like the beauty of a young woman, and she letting down her hair. God made the beauty of women, too, Marco Polo, as well as the beauty of the stars. Won't you please explain to me, Marco Polo? Why should Li Po say one thing and Saint Paul another?"

"But Golden Bells, Saint Paul is inspired of God."

"But Li Po is inspired of God, too, Marco Polo. You mustn't be thinking little of Li Po. He is fat and old and drunken, but when he sings, Marco Polo, it is the song of the wandering stars. But why must not the young men look at the young women, Marco Polo? Why must they not look with their eyes?"

"It will be hard for me to tell you, Golden Bells—"

"Look at me now, Marco Polo. Lift up your eyes and look into my eyes. Is there evil in me, Marco Polo, that your eyes should avoid me as the fox avoids the dog? Or maybe I am not beautiful. Maybe they told me wrong because I was a king's daughter, and they would not have me think little of myself. Maybe I am not beautiful, Marco Polo, maybe I hurt your eyes.—"

"Ah, Golden Bells, the little horned moon is not more beautiful."

"Then why must not the young men look at the young women, Marco Polo? You are here to instruct me. Won't you tell me why?"

"Maybe—maybe—maybe it is for fear of sin, Golden Bells."

"Sin? Sin! Why should there be sin? I know sin, Marco Polo. They have warned me against it since I crept upon the floor. There are two sins. There is meanness, Marco Polo, and there is cruelty; and those are the only sins. I know your heart, Marco Polo; there is no meanness there. You would not have come here were you mean. The mean do not travel afar for other people. And cruelty! Surely you would not be cruel to me, Marco Polo. You would not be cruel to anybody, dear Marco Polo. You would not be cruel to me?"

"Cruel to you, little Golden Bells! How could I be cruel to you?"

"But the sin, Marco Polo?"

"I don't know, Golden Bells. I don't know."

XIX

And one dusk the moon rose over the Chinese garden, and Marco Polo finished telling her of what John saw on Patmos and he an old man . . .

" *'Veni, Domine Jesu.*

" *'Gratia Domini nostri Jesu Christi cum omnibus vobis. Amen!'* "

"It is very difficult, Marco Polo. I don't quite understand."

"I don't quite understand myself, Golden Bells. But that is all I can tell you. But you will understand more," he said. "My mission is finished now, and I will go back. I will stop at the court of Prester John, and he will send a bishop surely or some great cardinal to baptise you and to teach you the rest."

"You will go back?" A great pain stabbed her. "I never thought, somehow, of you as going back."

"I have come on a mission, Golden Bells, and I must go back."

"There is a woman, maybe, in Venice —" And she turned her head away from him and from the moon.

"I would not have you thinking that, Golden Bells. There is none in Venice has duty from me. And if the queen of the world were there, and she pledged to me, I could never look at her, and I after knowing you, Golden Bells!"

"Is it money, Marco Polo?" she whispered in the dusk. "It is maybe your uncle and your father are pressing you to return. Let you not worry then, for my father the great Khan will settle with them, too. There is not a horse in all Tartary that your uncle cannot have, nor a woman, either. And your father can have all the jewels of the treasury, and all the swords, too, even the sword with which my father conquered China. My father will give him that if I ask. Only let you not be leaving this moonlit garden."

"Dear Golden Bells, it isn't that; but I came here for converts—"

"Oh, Marco Polo, listen! There is a folk at Kai-fung-fu, and they are an evil folk and a cowardly folk, and my father abhors them. I shall ask my father to send captains of war and fighting men to convert them to your faith, Marco Polo, or lop off their heads. And we can send a few hundreds to the Pope at Rome, and he will never know how they were converted, and he will be satisfied. Only let you not be going away from me in my moonlit garden. You will only be turning to trade, Marco Polo, and marrying a woman. Let you stay here in the moonlit garden!"

"Ah, little Golden Bells, there is no place in the world like your moonlit garden. There is no place I'd be liefer than in the moonlit garden. But little Golden Bells, I set out in life to preach the Lord Jesus crucified. It was for that I came to China."

"Let you not be fooling yourself, young Marco Polo. Let you not always be ascribing to God the things that are mine. You did not come to preach to China, you came to see me, and your mind stirred up with the story the sea-captain told, of me playing 'Willow Branches' by the Lake of Cranes. O Marco Polo, before you came there were the moon and the sun and the stars, and I was lonely. O Marco Polo," she cried, "you wouldn't go, you couldn't go! What would you be doing in cold Venice, far from the warm moonlit garden."

"Sure, I'll be lonely, too, little Golden Bells, a white monk in a monastery, praying for you."

"But I don't want to be prayed for, Marco Polo." She stamped her foot. "I want to be loved. And there you have it out of me, and a great shame to you that you made me say it, me that was desired of many, and would have no man until you came. And surely it is the harsh God you have made out of The Kindly Person you spoke of. And 'tis not He would have my heart broken, and you turning yourself into a crabbed monk. And how do you know your preaching will convert any? 'Tis few you converted here. Ah, I 'm sorry, dear Marco Polo; I shouldn't have said it, but there is despair on me, and I afraid of losing you."

" 'Tis true, though. I have nothing, nobody to show."

"You have me. Amn't I converted? Amn't I a Christian? Marco Polo, let me tell you something. I said to my father I wanted to marry you, and I asked him if he would give you a province to govern, and he said, 'Sure and welcome.' And I asked him for Yangchan, the pleasantest city in all China. And he said, 'Sure and welcome, Golden Bells.' And I told him we would be married, and go there and govern his people kindly. And you wouldn't shame me before my own father, and all the people of China. You couldn't do that, Marco Polo. Marco Polo,"—she came toward him, her eyes shining,—"let you stay!"

"Christ protect me! Christ guide me! Christ before me!"

"Marco Polo!"

"Christ behind me!"

"The moon, Marco Polo, and me, Golden Bells, and the nightingale in the apple tree!"

"Christ on my right hand! Christ on my left! Christ below me!"

Her arms were around his neck, her cheek came close to his.

"Marco Polo! Marco Polo!"

"Christ above me!"

"My Marco Polo!"

"O, God! Golden Bells!"

And he put his arms around her, and his cheek to hers, and all the battle and the disappointment and the fear and the strangeness went out of him. And down by the lake the wee frogs chirruped, and in the apple tree the nightingale never ceased from singing. And they stayed there shoulder to shoulder and cheek to cheek. And the moon rose higher. And it seemed only a moment they were there, until they heard the voice of Li Po in the garden.

"Are you there, Golden Bells? Are you there at all, at all? For two hours I've been hunting and couldn't get sight or sign of you. I have the new song, Golden Bells. For a long time I was dumb, but a little while ago the power came to me, and I have the new song, Golden Bells, the marrying song . . ."

XX

"Thus far," said Malachi of the Long Glen, "the story of Marco Polo."

"That is a warm story, Malachi of the Glen, a warm and coloured story, and great life to it, and Golden Bells is as alive to me as herself there by the fire, and I can see Marco Polo as plain as I can see my cousin Randall, and he playing with the dogs . . ."

"If they weren't real and live and warm, what would a story be, Brian Oge, but a jumble of dead words? A house with nobody in it, the poorest thing in the world."

"But Marco Polo came back to Venice, Malachi, and fought in the sea-wars."

"There's more to tell, Brian Oge. But sometimes I wonder shouldn't the best part of the story be kept to yourself. The people aren't as wise as they used to be, brown lad. The end of a story now is a bit of kissing and courting and the kettle boiling to be making tea.

"But the older ones were wiser, Brian Donn. They knew that the rhythm of life is long and swinging, and that time doesn't stop short as a clock. Sure, what is a kiss from the finest of women but a pleasant thing, like a long putt sunk, or the first salmon of the year caught like a trout, or the ball through the goal before the whistle blows? And there's many a well-filled belly over a hungry soul.

"But a story is how destiny is interwoven, the fine and gallant and the tragic points of life. And you mustn't look at them with the eyes of the body, but you must feel with the antennas of your being. Now, if you were to look at the Lord Jesus with physical eyes, what would it be but a kindly, crazy man and He coming to a hard and bitter end? Look at it simply, and what was the story of Troy but a dirty row over a woman?

"But often times the stories with the endings that grocer's daughters do not be liking are the stories that are worth while. And the worthwhile stories do be lasting. Never clip a story halfways because the Widow Robinson doesn't like to have her mind disturbed, and she warming her breadth at the fire. The Widow Robinson may have a white coin to buy a book with, and think you're the grand author entirely and you pleasing her. But the Lord God, who gave you the stories, will know you for a louse.

"I call to your mind the stories of the great English writer—the plays of the Prince of Denmark, and the poor blind king on the cliff, and the Scottish chieftain and his terrible wife. The Widow Robinson will not like those stories, and she will be keeping her white coin . . . But those stories will endure forever . . .

"I will now tell you of Marco Polo, and him leaving China . . ."

XXI

"You must see him now as he was seventeen years after he had come to China, and fourteen years after his wife, little Golden Bells, had died, a lean figure of a man, with his hair streaked with gray, a lean, hard face on him and savage eyes, and all the body of him steel and whalebone from riding on the great Khan's business, and riding fast and furious, so that he might sleep and forget; but forgetting never came to him . . . You might think he was a harsh man from his face and eyes, but he was the straight man in administering justice, and he had the soft heart for the poor—the heart of Golden Bells. He was easily moved to anger, but the fine Chinese people never minded him, knowing he was a suffering man. Though never a word of Golden Bells came from his mouth, barring maybe that line of Dante's, the saddest line in the world, and that he used to repeat to himself and no one there:

> . . . " 'la bella persona
> *Che mi fu tolta . . . che mi fu tolta';* who was taken from me; Taken! Taken from me!"

And oftentimes a look would come over his face as if he were listening for a voice to speak—listening, listening, and then a wee harsh laugh would come from him, very heartbreaking to hear, and whatever was in his hand, papers or a riding-whip, he would pitch down and walk away . . .

He had just come in from the borders of the Arctic lands, from giving the khan's orders to the squat, hairy tribes who live by the icy shores, and had come to the garden by the Lake of Cranes, the garden where the Golden Bells of singing and laughter were dumb this armful of years, and he was alone, and the listening look was on his face, when there came Kubla and Li Po and the old magician . . . Now Kubla was very old, so old he could hardly walk, and very frail, and Li Po was very old, too, and gray in the face, and sadder in the eyes than ever, and the magician's white beard had grown to his knees, but there was no more humour in his eyes . . . And Marco Polo helped the old Khan to sit down.

"Oh, sir, why did you come to me? Sure I was going to you the moment I had changed my riding-clothes . . . Sir, you should have stayed in your bed . . ."

"There was something on my mind, Marco, and the old do be thinking long to get things off their mind."

"What can I do sir?"

"Marco, my child, you mustn't take what I say amiss. But I want you to be going back, to be going back to Venice."

"Sir, what have I done to dissatisfy you? In all my embassies have I been weak to the strong or bullying toward the weak? Does an oppressed man complain of injustice, does a merchant complain of being cheated, or a woman say she was wronged?"

"Now, Marco of my heart, didn't I say not to be taking it amiss? Is there anyone closer to me nor you, or is it likely I'd be listening to stories brought against you? It's just this. I'm an old and tired man, Marco Beag, and in a week or a moon at most I'm due to die, so the *Sanang* tells me. Don't be sorry, son. Be glad for me. Life has been a wee bit too long.

"And now, son dear, I want to tell you. You've been closer to me than my own sons, and you've been the dear lad. And there's not one man in all China can say you did a harsh or an unjust thing; but, my dear son, 'tis just the way of people; there's a power of hard feeling against you in this land, you being a stranger and having stood so high.

"So when I'm dead, dear son, there's many would do you an injury, and treat you badly; aye, in our family itself, though they smile on you now. Let you be going now, Marco. I'll miss you to close my eyes for me, but my heart will be lighter. It will so. I couldn't sleep easy, and you ill treated in this land of mine. You ask him, too, Li Po."

"Ah, sir," Marco laughed,—"and, Li Po, what is ill treatment to me? Sorrow's my blood brother. What I've suffered! Do you think I could suffer more?"

"I know, Marco, I know."

"Don't you think I suffer now, sir? Fourteen years she's dead now, the wee one who lay by my side in sleep. And never a word and never a sign. In the house where we were married I can see the pool and the willows and the hibiscus, but there is never a token of her," he broke out. "The leaves of trees cover the pavilion, the hair of the musicians is silver, and dust is on the blue and white tiles. And she never comes to comfort me. I can't sleep with waiting. The stars never seem to wane, and the hoar frost comes on the grass, and I'm always waiting. Christ! why should I go back? I've forgotten Venice. I've even forgotten my God for her!"

"*Sanang*," says Kubla Khan to the magician, "couldn't you do something for this poor lad?"

It was now dusk in the garden by the Lake of Cranes . . .

"I don't need any damned wizard to bring my wife to me," raged Marco Polo. "If she were to come, she would come, and I in the dark of the moon and the moorfowl calling. She would have come because my heart needed her." And he raged through the dusk by the Lake of Cranes . . .

"Now, Marco, dear lad, don't be flying off again, but remember that there is science needed to all things. And think, too, that maybe she was not permitted. The older we get, the more we understand the destiny that rules all things, with now a nudge, with now a leading finger, with now a terrible blow over the heart, and what we think at twenty-five was a trifling accident, at seventy-five we know to have been the enormous gesture of God. We are not asked when we like to be born, Marco, nor is it up to us when to die.

"And again, Marco, consider. If she were to have come to you in the dark of the moon-time, in the strange mystic hours when you can hear eternity tick like a clock, your eyes would have been not on this world, but the next. Your look would have been vacant that's now keen to discover injustice. Your body would have been flabby that's now whalebone and steel. And there would have been no memory of you in China, that's now like sweet honey in the mouth.

"Would a wee dead spirit be proud of a man, Marco, and he just crying, crying, crying, and letting the days go by while even the brown bee works, and even the grass grows that cattle may fatten and men eat? She might be sorry, but would there be pride on her? Even a dead woman wants a strong man.

"Now, I'm not saying that the silent dead should not have a voice in our affairs when we need them. But they have wisdom, else what is the use of having died? And if the *Sanang* can bring her, she'll come now and join with us in asking you, now being the time she's needed.

"Child, be guided by us three ancient men. I have lived long and have knowledge of the world. Li Po has lived long and has knowledge of the heart. The *Sanang* has lived long, and knows the secrets of the dead. If to our three voices, who love you, there is added a sign from Golden Bells, will you leave China?"

"If there is a sign from her I'll leave China," said Marco Polo.

And it was dusk in the Garden by the Lake of Cranes.

XXII

The *Sanang* came over to Marco Polo.

"Give me the black tress that's over your heart."

And Marco Polo undid his coat and his undercoat and his fine sark and took out the perfumed hair, and gave it to the *Sanang*.

"Let you sing a little song, Li Po," the magician said, "the way she'll be hearing and come. I have part of her here, and let you put in the garden the atmosphere she loved." And Li Po took his lute and plucked gently at the strings.

"The swish of your silken skirt is discontinued," he sang,
"And the grass grows through the broken hearth stone,
And your room that was so warm and swept is cold and mouldy.
But he, the beloved of your heart, clings on,
A fallen leaf in the chink of a door, In the chink of a closed door!"

And it was dusk in the garden, and the voice of Li Po broke, and his lute stilled, and the old Emperor breathed his aged gentle breathing, and the *Sanang* said his secret terrible formulas, and Marco Polo was tense as a hunting dog.

And suddenly at the end of the garden, in the perfumed Asian dusk, there was a beam like moonlight, and into the soft ray of it trod Little Golden Bells, with her wee warm face, and her wee warm hands, and her hair dark as a cloud, and her eyes pleading, pleading . . .

"Go now, Marco Polo, please go!" Her lips made the words, but no sound came to him.

"Oh, Golden Bells, Golden Bells!" he rushed forward, but the moonlight of no moon faded, and there was nothing, and he dropped on his knees sobbing in the dusk by the Lake of Cranes . . .

XXIII

And after a while he got up from his knees and set his teeth on his sobbing and threw his head back and squared his shoulders and notched his belt and faced the three ancient men.

"Well," he said, "that's that."

He went over and knelt and kissed the Khan's hand.

"You'll be seeing her soon, sir, you'll be telling her . . . everything . . ."

"Yes, son, I'll tell her."

Then he patted the *Sanang* on the shoulder, and "Thanks!" said he, simply, and he took Li Po's hand in both his, and they looked at each other for a moment and no words came to either.

"Well," he says at length, "I'll be hitting the road then. I'll not say goodbye to any of you. I'll be seeing you all pretty soon again. There's a war on between Venice and the Genoese, and where that's hottest you'll find me, and the quicker my end, the better I'll be pleased. But it would be like my luck," he said bitterly, "not to be killed, but to be taken prisoner and to end my life in some lousy jail. Oh, well, we'll hope for the best." He laughed. "So—so long !"

And the four of them looked at one another, trying to smile, and great grief on them.

"China will miss you, my son," said old Kubla.

"It's nothing to how I'll be missing China," said Marco Polo. "Venice! It's only a sound to me. I'll be an exile in the city of my birth. But what's the use of complaining? If it's go, it's go. But it'll be funny," said he. "My body will be there, but my heart and mind will be in China. There'll be a gray eye always turning to

China, and it will never see China ... Queer! ... All the voices and all the instruments in Saint Mark's, and in my ears the little drums of China ... All the sunlight will be glinting on the Grand Canal, but the little rain of China—the little rain of China will be falling in my heart ...

"Ah, well, if it's go, it's go. I 'd better be hitting the road. So ... I'll say good-by for the present ... and ...

"Oh, my God Almighty! ..."

TILL END
OF
MESSER MARCO POLO